Please Tell Me If The Grass Is Greener

Joylynn M. Jossel

c. Copyright 1998 by END OF THE RAINBOW projects
Library of Congress Catalog Number: 00-192939

In-house Editing by Angela Reese
Angela812@msn.com

Photographs by Darett Barber
Darettbarber@hotmail.com

Website designed by Herb Baldwin
bigdawg_madhops@yahoo.com

Published in 2001 by
End of the Rainbow Projects
Post Office Box 298238
Columbus, OH 43229
614-806-6204
www.JoylynnJossel.com

Printed in the United States of America

Acknowledgements

Dedicated with love to The Creator, Mom, Dad, Nick (Bang), Ran-Ran, Hennessey, Fonda, Sisters, Grandparents, Aunts, Uncles, Cousins, Nieces, Nephews and Friends.

Love, Joylynn

Special Acknowledgment to Jeff Johnson, Sue Duffy and Nancy Flowers Wilson: Thank you for your help in packaging my gift :-)

Please Tell Me If The Grass Is Greener

Joylynn M. Jossel

I once heard someone criticize black writers for writing of drugs, rape, prostitution, murder, gangs and stealing. I am aware that such occurs not only in the lives of people of color but also in the lives of "people". The criticism alone reflects one's cowardliness to face the daily struggles of the people, and even worse, the weakness to stand up and acknowledge them.

My writings are not to insinuate that the lives of people of color wholly consist of violence and turmoil. These stories are my life, your life and ours. Although influenced by reality, the characters in my writings are merely fictional.

So with much respect I ask that if you are a coward and if you are weak, please place this book back on the shelf. No offense, but it was not written for you.

The Author

TABLE OF CONTENTS

Even Snowflakes Have Flaws……………………..……....Page 1

Eyes Like Mine ……………………………………..........Page 11

Sweet Potato Pie…....………………...…....................….Page 21

What Goes Around………….………...…...……………Page 31

Nothin' Worse Than an Unmade Bed…...…………........Page 43

Daddy's Little Girl………...……………….……………...Page 53

You Ever Seen A Grown Man Cry…..……………....….Page 63

Please Tell Me If The Grass Is Greener

A Collection of Short Stories

Even Snowflakes Have Flaws

Joylynn M. Jossel

*E*verybody thinks I'm going nowhere. They don't tell me this personally, but I can see it in their eyes. They talk about me behind my back, while to my face, they tell me lies.

"Zleeka, you've just made a few wrong turns in life, but someday your road is going to straighten out." Half the time I don't even think people know what they're talking about. I've been places most have never been nor would care to go. I've been places where people have had to step on me because I was so low.

It all started when I began doing drugs and selling my soul for a few minutes of high. The faster I would run from the devil to abandon my debt, the closer I found myself by the devil's side. That is what a drug is, the devil in pure disguise. I know this now, but it has taken me a long time to realize.

I always hooked up with the wrong crowd or men who only

loved me enough to turn me out. I found myself living foul without any hesitations or doubts. At the drop of a dime I was willing to do the time for any petty little crime. My lifestyle didn't scare me any; as a matter of fact it became less of a challenge. Everything would eventually get old, but I knew there was new dirt out there to balance.

When things got rough I'd pack a bag and leave home without a clue as to where I was going. There was never any reason to stick around with my bad attitude and my bad doings. During one of my journeys me and this man by the name of Duddy got involved. Duddy was the only man to truly love me, but we parted with problems that were never resolved.

My heart knew that Duddy really loved me even though he was from a much higher class. Nonetheless, my head worked on getting what it could from Duddy fast. I figured Duddy was stupid and easy to take for a ride or else why would he be bothered with me? I was nothing, felt like nothing, looked like nothing, and this wasn't hard to see.

Duddy would tell me to look at myself in the mirror, and he would always guarantee, that I would see the most beautiful woman in the world that there ever was to see: A naturally darkened tone with no make-up or help from even the sun's brightest ray, full figured lips, dark brown eyes, and versatile strands of hair to display; Strong bones and wide hips to support such a lovely foundation; The black woman, the most beautiful woman that ever existed across the nation.

I wanted to love Duddy back but how could I have possibly loved someone else? I know that one should love thy neighbor, but first one must love thyself. I stole from Duddy even though he was always willing to give. People say a leopard never changes its spots and this is how I had always lived. I never wanted anyone to feel as though I owed them something because it gets tiresome paying the fare. Duddy was just another one of my victims and at the time I didn't care.

Pop-bellied with Duddy's offspring, for an abortion I collected his money. I fed the dough to my veins without a care about the creature growing inside my tummy. Duddy got suspicious as my belly still began to grow. So again, I packed a bag and went on my way so that Duddy would never truly know. I didn't know what I was going to do or how I could use being pregnant to my advantage. On the streets, though, I learned how to get money from a couple whom was disadvantaged.

The warmth from the baby's body created a steam as he was lifted from between my legs. At the last minute I changed my mind, but all I could do was lay in that alley and beg. The money that laid beside me had taken the place of my biological child, who I knew would grow up someday to make a disadvantaged couple proud. That's how I justified trading the baby for money that didn't get me far. Soon enough I ended up sleeping on the streets and in the back seat of unlocked cars.

I was in the worse parts of town, where the pop would wake me from my sleep. My heart would race so fast. The crying would soon pass. Sometimes I wasn't sure about the pop. I never got close enough to know when it was being imitated. All I knew is that another one of my brothers had been eliminated...when I heard the pop.

I wasn't bothered by the fact that I would get arrested for panhandling, which caused me to be thrown in jail. Rather than sleep another night on the streets I'd rather spend the night in a cell. In jail is where I met Honey, a prostitute who taught me everything about turning tricks. She showed me where to buy my clothes and where to get my hair fixed.

Unique of "Unique's Hair Salon" is where all the hookers and queens would go in the neighborhood. Unique had that special knack to make even the most unattractive person look good. Unique always took care of business and she still does to this very day. She knew how to get the job done by knowing what to say:

"Come in and take a chair, and don't be cryin' the blues. You're the client and I have the license so don't be tellin' me what to do. So what if my hair is messed up. Don't you be worryin' 'bout me. If we plan on getting you together it will cost extra 'cause magic tricks ain't free. Don't call yourself a regular, then show up every blue moon, or make an appointment for 11 o'clock and come striding in at noon. Don't be chair hoppin' to every shop up and down the street, then come back to me with your hair all raggedy and blame it all on me. Don't bring me no magazine pictures because trust me you are no model. Don't bring your kids either. I don't have time to waste while you feed your baby a bottle. If you want to go through life lookin' good, then, child, you better listen. I'm not going to let you look like no fool because I'm your friend, but most importantly, I'm your beautician."

Unique would have me looking so good that I had regular Johns, which is nothing to be proud of. I was just having sex with men for money, not for love. I was lucky, but I learned the hard way that women like me could end up dead in ditches. When I went after a John for not paying his toll I ended up with 627 stitches. He sliced my mouth, my nose, my ears, and the blade sliced my tongue after entering my jaw. Then he sliced my shoulders, my arms, my hands, and my fingers until I finally fought him off. It wasn't until I saw my blood surrounding me that I knew I had to make a change. My blood was as red as any other human beings, so why was I living so inhumane?

I spent months healing in the hospital, and at the same time I was building my master plan. I planned to find me a decent job and never have to depend on the likes of any man. I was shooting for the stars with a sure guarantee to miss, but as spoken, it is better to shoot for the stars and miss than to shoot for the gutter and hit.

I honestly tried. I found a clerical job working for a small business with all whites. I had to change the way I walked and talked. I went from fish net panty hose to coffee brown tights. I couldn't get used to the atmosphere though. I was in a totally different world. I was reminded of the saying my grandmother would recite when I was a little girl:

"I have an advantage over you. I do. Even though my eyes aren't blue, I can talk like you, but my color is true. How did this advantage come about, now that I am allowed near your spout? To be like you I have no choice. This is your world. This is your voice. I can relate to your humor but to mine you frown. My advantage allows me survival in any part of town. I'm not trying to be like you. I simply enjoy fooling you with the advantage I have over you. I do."

My clerical job didn't last long. I got back to doing some of the same old things. I waited tables in a lounge where my sister, Teal, used to sing. My sister could sing better than any of those girls in En Vogue, Whitney, or Mariah. Then one day she met a man who she swore was her very own Messiah. She fell for him hook, line, and sinker. She was head over heals in love. I knew he wouldn't stay around long because he fit the "player" profile like a glove. Teal couldn't see this. I guess the old cliché is true about love being blind. I remember the night he left her. I sat with her and she cried the entire time. When my sister and I were young we were close, but we hadn't been close for years. But at that time we had something in common, cold-lonely tears.

I left my sister alone that night because I had a calling from my addiction. When I returned the next morning I found my sister with a bullet through her head. Her brain was blown all over the kitchen. I didn't sleep for days or eat for days. I just sat and looked at Teal's picture that was on the shelf. My mother told me that I couldn't have stopped her, therefore, I shouldn't blame myself. But what did people expect me to do once Teal was gone? I felt as though I couldn't possibly go on. What my sister was thinking at the time I couldn't help but wonder as I was reminded of her fate by the crack of thunder. I should have held her tight and whispered in her ear that everything was all right. God didn't even give me a sign. Now the clock still ticks, but there is no more time. The nights seemed to be the worse when memories alone can't quench the thirst. I probably shouldn't have felt guilty, but still I asked myself what had I done as I indulged on the salt from the tears on my tongue. I didn't know what I would do once Teal was gone, but I cried, wailed, and appealed, then I moved on.

After my sister's death I moved back home with my mom and dad. I lived on government assistance and sat around the house feeling bad. I contacted an old partner of mine who got me a legitimate job that afforded me a car. My father threw me out the house when he found out the job was stripping in a bar. I couldn't seem to win for losing, but I thought it would be different since the job was legit. But my goal to earn money, and not steal it, had morals hanging over it.

I thought my boss at the strip club was a pretty decent guy when he put me up at his place. He gave me a month to get myself together, so I was to stay on a temporary and platonic basis. My stay turned out to be even shorter because one night when he came in late, he entered my room in a drunken rage and what I wouldn't give him he managed to take.

I couldn't understand why God had mapped out for bad things to happen to me. I questioned why I should even believe in this God I've never seen. But to disbelieve in God for that reason would have been insane. I had never seen the wind, but I knew it was there, nor had I ever seen pain.

Right now it is so hard to go on. I can't describe the lack of will I have to live. Something in my life has to change. Something has got to give. I can't expect God to bail me out of my troubles, most of them of which I have caused. God has witnessed everything from my manipulating and my destruction, to my breaking laws.

I sought out many types of resources to help me change. There was some assistance, but no one really thought my lifestyle was wrong. Society has been programmed to believe that on the streets or in jail is where people like me belong.

I built the walls to my own prison. There is no one else to blame. Now I must find a way to free myself. I have to break the chains. But what is freedom really? Is it something I can look out the window and see? Will it be walking barefoot on the grass or climbing up a tree? If I call to it "FREEDOM", will it abruptly respond? Will it haven itself at dusk and rejuvenate at dawn? Can I reach out and touch freedom, hold it in my hand? If I acquaint all my heartaches, will it understand? I would love to smell this freedom of which I have been told. I fear I might not even know it was there if it were right under my nose. If I could ladle up freedom, I wouldn't hesitate to take a taste. The world would be able to see the expression of freedom on my face. I hope that all of those who find freedom will love, adulate, and adore it, but most importantly I hope they will tell freedom that I too am looking for it.

When I think of the 25 years I have wasted, my stomach pains of rotten meat spoiled by the summer's sun. I wish for all this hurt to end, but I know that self-healing has just begun. If I could turn back the hands of time there is plenty I would change. Simply wishing for an unrealistic solution won't take away this pain. Now my only friends seem to be regret, guilt, and blame. I never knew until now how much remorse my heart could retain.

My mother tells me that if I stare out at the world full of hopes and dreams, the closer I get to them the further away they may seem. But that I shouldn't get discouraged, is what my mother tries to teach. She said even though I may not be able to see my dreams they are always within my reach. There's a song she used to sing as well, "*Hmmm. I been buked and I been scorned. I been talked about. Shows I'm born.*" Those words ended up reflecting me. Believe it or not they have helped me to see. It is time to wake up. It is time to live. It is time to stop taking. It is time to give.

The road ahead is going to be the roughest road I have traveled yet. I'm going after something I have never had for myself and that is respect. I know because of where I come from and where I've been people think I don't have a chance in the world. Maybe after hard times some people give up on life, but definitely not this girl. One day I am going to be someone others will speak good of because I'm going to make it. I'm going to gain some strength and gain some hope and not let anyone take it. It's going to take time but all good things to those who wait (all good things come to an end). Contradictions of how life is supposed to be never seem to end. But I am going to make do with whatever is dished out to me, so that whatever is meant to be done in my life will be done by me.

Just when the world started to crumble around me suddenly it is rebuilt. The rose that stands tall in my vase today, yesterday was wilt. I am going to be proof that if the path one chooses to lead turns out to be a bitter way, that they can turn back and start fresh in the morning because tomorrow is a brand new day. I am going to shoot through all barriers and obstacles without taking the slightest pause. Don't expect me to be perfect though, because even snowflakes have flaws.

Eyes Like Mine

Joylynn M. Jossel

I'm sitting here looking into the eyes of a child who was not created by me but who is now mine. I have never even been one to baby-sit, but I keep telling myself that everything is going to be fine. I never looked at a child as being anything more than a bother. Now here I am doing another man's job by being this child's father.

Don't get me wrong. I love this little boy as if he were my own. It scares me though, that someday he will be a black man out in this world alone. I see black men dying left and right; a knife through the heart or a bullet through the head. My mother used to tell me that the black man doesn't die, he's born dead.

Mother would repeat, "The doctors should snap the black man's neck at birth. A horse isn't even forced to suffer. The life of a black man doesn't get any better. It only gets rougher and rougher."

As a boy, these were the insults I would constantly hear because Mother was set on putting the black man down. I would some day grow to be a black man so I worried if Mother would then want me around. By being born a male I had already failed her in life. It was serendipity, but Mother's tongue prepared me for the fight.

I grew up with a fear of becoming a black man, so all my life I've tried exceptionally hard to do right. Sometimes the other brothers out there make me feel like it's a no win fight. If one black man robs a bank then that black man might as well be me. Because when I go on a job interview that black man is the only man they see. When a brother goes out and gets a white girl and turns her out on drugs, it is my honest brothers and myself who get labeled as losers and thugs.

I'm damn tired of defending myself for crimes of which I have not committed. If I ever cause fault to someone else's life, then I'd be man enough to admit it. But there's no need for me to be bitter. What's done is already done. Today all black men have a responsibility to do right. I'm not the only one.

Mother told me I wouldn't do right. She said I'd grow up to be exactly like my father. She said I'd find a good woman, beat that good woman, make babies, and continue life without a bother.

"You'll end up in jail," Mother said, "I can see you now all doped up and high. Your daddy wasn't nothin'. You ain't gonna be nothing so you might as well not even try."

I cried. Oh my God did I cry. The pain and sadness Mother had in her heart made me want to die. It was her own hurt she was releasing. It had nothing to do with me, except for the fact that she feared she alone couldn't raise a black man and this failure she didn't want to see.

Consequently, that is when my responsibility as a black man came into play. As much as Mother went through for me I wasn't going to let her see that day. I remember how my father would hit Mother (It's funny. I can't seem to picture my father's face). I can remember the occasions he would come home drunk and completely demolish the place.

Mother would call Big Mama and Pops (her parents). Pops would come over waving his gun. Everybody knew that it had no bullets in it, not a one. My father would relinquish anyway just to give Pops the gratification of protecting his family. Big Mama would preach to Mother that staying with my father was, in fact, sleeping with the enemy.

"But the boy, Big Mama," Mother would cry, "he needs his father. I can't raise him by myself."

"Honey-child," Big Mama would respond, "leave him with his daddy while you go out and seek your wealth."

Mother would peep around the corner at me. My head was down with my hands in the pockets of my pants. Then Mother would turn back to Big Mama and with no further doubt say, "I can't."

Ironically, my father was the one who ended up doing the leaving. He packed up his belongings and kissed Mother and me good-bye one summer evening.

Mother and my father had been together five years before my time plus my first five years on earth. "Elena," my father said to Mother, "I only see things getting worse. I haven't been man enough to stop hitting you or man enough to stop picking up a drink. But there is one thing I've been man enough to do and that, my dear, is to think. Your heart won't understand why I'm doing this and society will label me as a typical black man. But before I stay around and continue to hurt my family I'll cut off my right hand."

My father left. We never saw him again. He was gone without a trace. I remember the tears toppling from his eyes (It's funny though. I can't seem to picture my father's face).

I don't hold anything against my father. The best thing he could have done for us was to leave. In his own unacceptable by society way he set Mother and me free.

At such a young age I was left to be the man of the house. However, by the time I was in high school men had been in and out. I fought with these men. I talked to them anyway I pleased. I even cursed. Before I would let any man mistreat Mother I'd fearlessly die first.

Of course Mother didn't go for this. She would knock me upside my head. With tears of refuge I would cry to her that before a man mistreated her she'd see him dead.

"I can't wait until you're 18," Mother would say, "so you can get out of my house."

I never took those words to heart. Where I come from that came out of almost every mother's mouth.

After Mother and I would argue I'd go talk with Pops for a while. Listening to Pops' childhood stories always gave me a smile.

"Boy your mama is like a wounded Doe," Pops would always start off, "and she needs you by her side while she heals, so don't you go gettin' lost. There's a difference between *'lost'* and lost so listen to me boy."

By that time I knew Pops was setting up the path for his same old story:

> *"I was standing outside the grocery store when a woman asked, "Are you lost little boy? Why are you wandering about?"*
> *"No Mam. I'm just waiting for my mama," I said, "she said she'd be right out."*
> *As the woman walked on I contemplated over what sense of the word lost she meant. Had I lied to the woman outside the grocery store? On this my thoughts were spent. Am I recognized at all for who I am or am I just a shade of fear? Was this land really made for you and me? Do I really belong here? Do I care whether or not my brother lives or*

dies, or the same about myself? Will I have an equal opportunity to enjoy this country's great wealth? Do I know at all about my history or am I merited only on <u>his-story</u>? Should I strive to what may be a dead end not knowing what's in store for me? Where am I headed? I haven't the slightest idea. Will I be carried off by society's breeze? I had to find that woman outside the grocery store to set my mind at ease. I searched high and low for that woman. I had to get the truth to her at all cost. But I too had to hurry back to the grocery store or my mama would have thought I was lost."

Pops told that story to every brother in the neighborhood. He wanted to see all of us do good. I wanted to do good for myself more than anybody could ever dream. I wanted it for Mother, my family, and most importantly, I wanted it for me.

I made it up in my head that no matter what I'd keep my nose clean. On the other hand there was slinging dope and my profit, the dope fiend. Some brothers had Cadillacs, Mercedes Benzes, and phat gold chains for days. But none of those materialistic set ups could coerce me into changing my ways. Those high priced cars and fancy particulars carried an odor worse than any smell. The odor of a young brother in a 10' x 9' jail cell.

I don't put down the hustlers though. I don't condone what they do either. That loot weighing down their pockets only makes them weaker and weaker. I understand them wanting to make sure their family has a meal to eat each night. Slinging dope pays the bills and puts food on the table even though it's not right. Like I said, I don't put down the hustlers. Those brothers feel that they are doing what they have to do. I can't say anything bad against them because different circumstances could have turned me into a hustler too.

With all aside, my main goal was to soak up a lifetime worth of knowledge. I wanted to be the first one in my family to conquer that loophole called college. First I had to make it through high school, which in itself was a challenge. As always, there was that one person who it seems was put on earth to throw someone's dream off balance.

In my sophomore year of high school one of my teachers asked me to stand. She requested that I tell my peers what I wanted for myself as a man. I told them that I wanted to go to college as no one in my family had done before. This teacher looked at me and said, "Which university do you want to play basketball for?"

That single statement knocked me down a peg. It made me think about what I had failed to thus far. How else was I going to pay for college unless I tokened myself as a basketball star?

By the end of my senior year of high school I had an idle grade point average of 4.0. At graduation my Valedictorian speech earned me a standing ovation. In short, I stole the show. That fall I entered college on a full academic scholarship. My battle had just begun. In my optimistic thoughts the battle had already been won. I was living in the campus dorms. I had finally made it out on my own. I once had a fear that I'd never see that day. At that point in my life I thought nothing could go wrong.

But one day the school secretary came into the main lecture hall and tapped me upon my shoulder. I left the room with her and when I saw Big Mama and Pops my blood chilled colder and colder. All of a sudden there was this awful roar that echoed through the halls. Then this crying holler ricocheted off the walls. There was another awful roar and I recognized it this time. I realized that these chilling sounds had come from the voice box of mine.

That was when Big Mama had broken the news to me that Mother had been killed. The drive by bullet hadn't been meant for her, but I suppose it was God's Will.

Mother had walked to the mailbox only moments after an argument between two gangs had occurred. Before anyone knew it, shots were fired, and Mother's body lay dead on the curb.

Four weeks went by before I returned to school. My dorm mate had piled all my mail upon my bed. On top of the pile was a letter written by Mother and this is what it read:

Dear Braylee,
    We haven't talked for a while. It feels like it's been such a long time. As a matter of fact, it's been far too long. That's why I'm dropping you a line. I don't even know where to start. Baby, no matter what you might think you've always been my heart. I feel so distant from you. I guess it's a barrier that I created. But I've only just realized this now that we're separated.
    So many people have done wrong to me. So many people have tampered with my pride. Through it all you've been the only one by my side. For you, I don't know whether that was good or bad. Because you were the only one there, I took out all the anger on you that I had.
    I look back at all the things I've said to you and my eyes fill with tears. They weren't meant to be words of anger. They were words of my fears.
    You're in college now and I know you feel like you're on top of the world. You'll probably graduate with honors then go on to marry the perfect girl. You will have children and I'm sure you'll teach them well. I didn't teach you the things you needed to know. But look at you, who can tell?
    Baby, don't get your hopes up too high. I know what this world has to offer. They'll hand you your degree, dress you up in a suit, but still they'll see you as the culprit. You'll be an even bigger threat because you've attended college. The only thing worse than a black man to them is a black man with knowledge.

Well, good luck, Son. I'll let you go now. I don't want to keep you from studying those books. But one last thing, "I Love You, Son" no matter how sometimes things might have looked.

Mother

Mother had never said "I love you" to me, therefore I was never given the opportunity to say it back to her. There were times when I would sit and stare at Mother and get the urge to say "I love you" on the spur. I never did. That is the only act of cowardliness I can honestly admit. "I love you Mother! I love you Mother!" But now it's too late to say it.

Mother is gone. But she did leave behind the fruit of her priceless labor. Knowing that I, Mother's son, did right, is a message I'll communicate to my fruits to savor.

So here I sit looking into the eyes of a child who was not created by me but who is now mine. His eyes assure me that he too will grow to be a strong black man because he has eyes like mine.

Sweet Potato Pie

Joylynn M. Jossel

Sweet Potato Pie

  Today is the day that Eric and I are going to picnic together. One thing is for sure; we don't have to worry about the weather. And there won't be any outdoor animals trying to get in our food or pesky little insects to spoil the mood.

  I've made enough food for an army to feast. Eric is going to be so pleased, to say the least. I was up at the crack of dawn frying chicken. It looks like a caterer has been in my kitchen. I made macaroni, baked beans, and some other dishes for the side. I've even made Eric's favorite dessert, sweet potato pie.

  Eric loves my sweet potato pie. He never saves any for me. I make the pie by following my Great Grandma Barbara's recipe. My aunts tell me that Great Grandma Barbara could really cook up some food. But in order to enjoy the savoring rewards everyone had to listen to her rules:

*"Never be so rude
as to tell me how to prepare my food.
The fire ain't too high.
There ain't too much sugar in the pie.
The food don't have to be nutritious
just as long as it's delicious.
So shut up and sit down at the table
and grab yourself a ladle.
'Cause if there's gonna be any bitchin'
it's gonna be me cause it's my kitchen!"*

Everybody tells me that I cook just like Granny, that I can really throw down. Eric says that if I sold my pies, people would journey from all around. He says I should make them more often, not just on certain occasions. Eric complains that I only make them for him in accompaniment of an apology or his birthday celebration. Besides Eric's birthdays, I've made him a pie the time I wrecked his jeep. I made him a pie when a car hit his Rottweiler because I let it run into the street. As a matter of fact, one time I made the pie because of my guilty conscious. Every time I think of what I did, it makes my stomach nauseous.

It was two summers ago. Eric and I weren't married yet. But he was happy as could be when I told him I was pregnant. Being an unwed mother had never been in my life's plan. Just because I was pregnant was no reason to marry a man. I can't say I was the least bit happy. I didn't know what I was going to do. I hadn't planned on having children until after I had finished law school.

Then one weekend my little cousin and my niece spent the night at my house (they're about the same age). I never thought that in such a conversation the two were adroit enough to engage. I think they had been playing, then again, I remember it occurring over a bowl of cereal. The two were quiet at first, then out of the blue, my little cousin became quite trivial.

"Do you have a daddy?" my cousin asked my niece as I observed from the other room. My niece chuckled as she replied, "Yes, everybody has a daddy. Don't you?"

"But have you ever seen your daddy?" my cousin asked in disbelief.

"You ever seen your daddy?" my niece smartly replied as my cousin bowed his head in grief. My niece then continued to eat her breakfast and sooner or later my cousin lifted his head.

"Does he live with you?" was his comeback, "Does he and your mommy share a bed?"

"No, he lives with his girlfriend," my niece said, "Him and my mom aren't together anymore."

"And that still makes him your daddy?" my cousin asked as if he weren't too sure.

"Of course, stupid!" my niece answered, "He comes get me and gives my mom money from his check. When I'm not at his house he calls me all of the time. All daddies are suppose to do that."

My niece stood up after slurping down her milk. My cousin sat there picking at his cereal sadly. Before excusing herself, my niece asked, "Do you have a daddy?"

I interrupted them because I couldn't listen to them anymore. There was no way I was going to let the child inside me be born. If anything happened between Eric and me I'd be alone. And even worse I'd have to raise the child on my own.

So I got out Granny's recipe and baked Eric a sweet potato pie. As soon as I told him of the choice I had made he started to cry.

"From the first moment I met you, Jude," Eric cried, "you changed my entire life. I have been good and honest to you in order to earn you as my wife. We fell in love instantly and things have moved a little too fast. We haven't celebrated our union yet, but I know our love will last. You know how much I love you, Jude, and you know how much I care. I promise to never leave your side. No matter what, I'll always be there. I know you love me the same, but I guess it's natural for you to have doubts. As long as we support one another we can stick it out. I know it's your body, but after all is said and done, please remember that inside your body is the body of our daughter or son."

    I understood how Eric felt but still, I wanted to terminate the pregnancy. Eric said that committing such an act was raping our families of a legacy. There was nothing Eric could do or say to give me a change of heart. But he testified the entire drive to the clinic up until the time we parked.

    When we got out of the car we were rushed by protesters handing us pamphlets and carrying signs. When we entered the clinic we stood in the doorway while Eric pleaded unsuccessfully one last time.

    We sat in the clinic and waited until it was time for the procedure to take place. After it was over it took weeks before I could look Eric in the face. Even though Eric was against the abortion, as promised, he stood by my side. I don't remember whether or not he ever got around to eating that sweet potato pie.

    Maybe I shouldn't take the pie on the picnic. Eric will think something's wrong as soon as he sees it. It looks too good, though, to be put to waste. I couldn't dare make a pie without Eric getting a taste. I'll just leave it in the basket until after we've eaten and talked. That will give me time, without him being suspicious, to release my thoughts.

    I don't want to putrefy our picnic in any kind of way. Eric says looking forward to our picnic once a month is what gets him through the days. See, for the last 11 months Eric's being in jail has been really hard.

He was sentenced 10 to 25 years for killing a man in a bar. The man was an enemy of the friend Eric was with. When Eric saw the man pull out a gun, something in him clicked. Because when the man aimed the gun at Eric's friend's head, Eric busted his beer bottle, cut the man's throat, and watched him fall dead. So, for the last 11 months we've had picnics in the jail. Otherwise we communicate through phone calls and U.S. mail.

It's been hard for me as well, trying to be the supportive wife. But I've decided, in order to stay sane, I have to go on with my life. When I married Eric for good times and bad, I thought there would be more happy than sad.

I don't know how to tell Eric that I can no longer cope with his being in jail. I've never wanted to hurt him. I'd rather burn in hell. But I can't go on much longer pretending that our life is like a picnic. For months I've pretended and now it's time to be realistic.

I've been faithful to Eric, though often I desire a caressing touch. Except for our picnic once a month, I can only dream of Eric's passionate clutch. I've been confiding these feelings in Malik, an attorney who's worked at the firm for a while. At first we used to just go to lunch together, but lately we've become good pals. I'm afraid it's going to become more than that because I've noticed that an attraction now exists. After lunch, Malik and I have been departing with a kiss. But that's as far as it has gone and that's as far as I'll allow it to go. As long as I'm wearing my wedding band I'll never let my true lust show.

The one thing that confuses me is that my love for Eric is still as strong as before. But my feelings for Malik are, too, genuine. I can't keep separating my feelings anymore.

I find it so hard to obviate comparing things as secondary as Malik's and Eric's touch. And even more so the way their words are spoken and other lucid effects that don't really mean much. But worst of all, when I'm with Eric, it's hard to close my eyes and try to forestall from envisioning Malik's face, or grant strokes of unavailing kisses to Malik knowing that it's Eric's tongue I long to taste. When I'm with Malik sometimes I feel guilty because Eric is on my mind. But when I'm engaging in impassioned eventualities with Eric, I desire Malik the entire time. Still, I continue pretending, with Eric, to be what I tell him I'm all about. I wear this mask of confusion to bed each night praying of a contented way out.

The time has come. I have to tell Eric how I really feel. I haven't been playing games and that my love for him has always been real. By doing so, I'm being a real woman about the situation. Making love to another man on the down low would cause even greater devastation. So before it gets to the point where I'm being satisfied by another man's touch, I have to tell Eric because I'm his wife and I owe him that much.

Maybe I'm being selfish. Maybe I should just hang in there for my man. Or maybe I should let my true feelings for Malik show and hope that someday Eric will understand. But what if it's just the opposite? What if Eric becomes depressed? What if he hangs himself from a ceiling bar in order to meet his death? He's always told me he could never live without me, so would that make me a killer? I would then have made myself his weakness instead of his pillar.

I can't breathe. I'm suffocating. I can't believe this is happening again. Why do I keep putting my poor mind through this? This quandary has to end. Today is not going to be like the other times. I'm going to tell Eric how I feel for sure. My poor soul is weary and my brain is too drained to take anymore.

Oh, Allah, please give me a sign if this is really the right thing to do. Keep me from finding my car keys if it isn't. If it is, make my drive smooth.

No...maybe...yes. Yes it is! This is right. I can feel it in my heart. There is no way I can stay sound and continue to keep Eric in the dark.

I better hurry up. I don't want to keep Eric waiting too long. Especially now that I've psyched myself up to believe that what I'm doing isn't wrong.

Okay, I'm fine. I'm collected. I can make it. The drive is really not that far. I've got my ID and my keys, now I just need to load the food into the car. Why am I so worried anyway? Eric's probably known how I've felt each time he's looked into my eyes. But now I must go confirm his intuition with this sweet potato pie.

What Goes Around

Joylynn M. Jossel

There's a saying that some little girls grow up to be women while others grow up to be ho's. I've been single all 27 years of my life so a brotha like myself definitely knows. I've had my share of females, not tooting my own horn. It hasn't all been a bed of roses. There have been several thorns.

I must admit, though, that a lot of times I've brought grief upon myself. A sure way of doing so is assuming that a woman can place her feelings up on a shelf. Not saying that men don't have feelings, but ours are easier to hide. When females tell men that they only want to have fun (no relationship), we gladly push all feelings aside.

When it comes to having an understanding with women, men are like bulls in a China shop. Sometimes once a woman turns her feelings on she can't turn them off. Usually everything is cool until that intimate level is reached. Then the verbal contract to "just be friends" is null and void due to breach. Which reminds me of my situation with Angie, a girl I used to see. I told her that I dig her, but a serious relationship wasn't for me. She agreed to respect my feelings and promised that on them she wouldn't invade. It wasn't long though, before I found myself face down in the bed I had made.

I can't even lie about it. My initial intention was taking Angie to bed. I felt justified since I hit her off from the start versus playing silly games with her head. I didn't just have sex with her. I enjoyed her company so we did other things too. We'd go to the movies, to dinner, or what ever else she wanted to do.

What Angie and I had was cool, at least that's what I thought. Eventually, like a mouse in a trap, I was caught. Even though I had other female friends Angie really was my number one. But Angie felt that because I granted her most of my time she would eventually become the only one.

I mean, she was a beautiful woman, intelligent, had a good job, a nice house, and a car. But she just wasn't someone I had planned on building a committed relationship with by far.

I never set out to hurt her. That's why I made sure from the very start we had a mutual understanding. Like I said, it was all-good until she started getting jealous and demanding.

Angie got to the point where she wanted to be with me every day. She would come to my house unannounced, which started messing up my play. She was like an ant at a picnic. She just wouldn't stop bothering me. I was afraid one morning I'd look in the mirror and it would be her ass I'd see.

I was turned off even though Angie would've done anything to please me. But like my man Tupac said, and he was speaking the truth, "I don't want it if it's that easy." She was no longer a challenge, therefore my ego wasn't getting any exercise. The challenge is what makes it exciting; at least that's how it is in my eyes.

One night Angie dropped by when I had a lady friend over who I was trying to entertain. I thought I was going to have to call over an Exorcist because Angie cold went insane. Veins started popping out of her forehead and she started screaming at the top of her lungs. I thought she had been training with Mike Tyson after I saw the way she swung. She jabbed me and even pulled the weave out of my lady friend's head. This brawl could have gone on all night if 5-0 hadn't shown up when they did.

I didn't press charges on Angie. Instead, I told them to just let her be. But only under the condition that she stayed the hell away from me. For a while she still kept calling me like I was crack and she was the fiend. There would be a zillion messages with her begging and crying on my answering machine.

I really knew I had a case on my hands when she started threatening to scratch up my ride. I had worked hard for that 1998 Expedition so it was my true joy and pride. I couldn't understand why she was doing this. She and I were intimate but never were really a couple. That's when I learned that asking a woman to hubber her feelings is asking for trouble. I also learned something else as a result of Angie's and my altercation. That there is a dangerous copycat for love out there going under the alias of infatuation.

Not all women are Angies. There are those who wouldn't have it any other way. These women love the fact that they don't have to be bothered by the same guy every day. They have "Blockbuster," the one who takes them to the movie theater. Then there's the one that takes them out to eat, a.k.a., the "Caterer." There's "Saturday Night Live," the one who they shake it up with at the club. Then there's "Master" (as in MasterCard), the one who buys them anything they dream of. There's "1-800 Collect," the one who doesn't get any closer than the telephone.

Then there's "Fly Swatter," the one who gets to "hit it" when she doesn't want to be alone.

These are the women men have to keep their guard up with from the start. She is so smooth that, like the Pink Panther, she'll sneak up in a man's heart. Pink Panther won't play games or tell a man what he wants to hear. If they're compatible then the time she allots him is sincere.

Pink Panther keeps busy so don't sit by the phone hoping she'll be the cause of the ring. She won't pen in any dates on her scheduler either. First come first serve is her thing.

When I first met my Pink Panther, Michele was her name. I didn't start off being "Fly Swatter." I had to start by being Jack of all trades. But she let me know where I fit in and it was up to me to work my way up. Keeping in mind that the average Pink Panther only gives the man a couple of months. After that, if he doesn't learn his place, then like a miscellaneous pencil mark, he's erased. That lets her know that he moves too slow and won't be able to keep up with her pace.

Michele, Michele, Michele. Every time I say her name my mouth soaks with saliva. That girl blew my mind like a volcano blows lava. She had more class than a four-year university. That girl could get Satan to love her with that suave personality.

See, Michele had numerous male friends, but one would never know. She was the type who preferred to play the role versus actually be the ho. She seldom spent her dollars on a beautician and yet a hair was never out of place. She didn't wear bright eye catching make-up, but natural cosmetics that blended with her face. She had this aroma, her favorite oil, which to me was an aphrodisiac. When it came to her wardrobe, she looked good in anything on the rack.

Michele had attended college; as a matter of fact she had two degrees. She rubbed elbows with all walks of life and she never once thought she was any better than me. It didn't matter that Michele was the kind of girl who was out to have fun. She had this skill of making a man feel as though he was her only one.

I started finding myself wondering who Michele might be with when the two of us were apart. Before I knew it, or could prevent it, she was all up in my heart. I started telling her how much I liked her, which was a big mistake. To a girl like Michele, the game is over when there's nothing more at stake. Michele feared men falling in love with her because she knew that would cause a change. It takes away from the fun when new rules are added in the middle of the game.

I honestly could have spent the rest of my life with Michele, but I couldn't stop her from doing what she was doing. And just like the Pink Panther once the mystery was solved, she moved on.

The bad part about it is that I ended up sleeping with, Tasha, one of Michele's close friends. Tasha had always flirted with me so she heard opportunity knocking when Michele and I came to an end.

A girl like Tasha ain't nothing but a mattress, something to lay on at night. And even though Michele and I were through, Tasha's sleeping with me still wasn't right. I thought not sleeping with a friends ex was an unspoken rule. I'm not saying that it was all Tasha's fault. I was wrong too.

Depending on the circumstances though, sometimes it's different for women than it is for men. Especially if the female's just a chicken head, then the guy becomes a hen. So not to alter the assembly line I put Tasha in the recycling bin. In other words, when I was finished with her I passed her on to a friend.

I know that sounds cold and everybody probably thinks I'm a dog. But if a female stands herself up for that, then she has to prepare for the fall. A man won't do any more to a female than that female allows. The easiest targets to get over on are the pussycats on the prowl.

Usually the pussycats can be found lined up in the club like dominos. Don't get me wrong. I'm not saying that all females who go to the clubs are ho's. Some go to get their groove on simply because they love to dance. Some go to get their drink on while conversing with their friends. Then there's the ones just standing around with price tags hanging from their clothes. Their mammas are watching their babies, and how many the Lord only knows.

The pussycats are like diamonds in the rough to an alcohol filled man. All he has to do is buy a drink, talk some shit, and BOOM, a one-night stand. If the putty-tat ain't good, then she definitely won't get a call in the future. But if the man remembers her the next day, then more than likely he'll recruit her. Recruiting the pussycat isn't much work at all, but there's an expense that comes along with it. The man has to get her hair done, give her money, or buy an outfit each time he hits it.

Some people might think that men who shell out dough to these women are crazy. But how these men take ownership of these pussycats is amazing. For every dollar the man spends on her he's increasing the value of his stock. Before no time at all the pussycat is owned and bought.

The man gets it when he wants it and how he wants because the pussycat knows that it's her duty. She can't complain or turn him down because she's the one who put the price tag on her booty. That just goes to show that everything in life can be bought for the right price. It's sometimes not knowing the form in which payment must occur that's not so nice.

In actuality it's a power struggle between the two. The man gets what he wants and the pussycat gets what she wants too. The man plays the female for her pussycat and she plays him for his wealth. They each walk away from the relationship not realizing that each only played themselves.

I met a girl like that once, Paula, but she not only wanted me to spend money on her. She had two kids she wanted me to buy stuff for, her eight-year-old son and her five-year-old daughter. I ain't lying; this story is for real. She told me that she and her kids were a package deal.

I could understand Paula because if I had kids they too would be a part of me. But I wouldn't include them in my money making scheme. But that's how she was, if I took her out to eat, her *Be Be's* joined us as well. She said "my kids are just as hungry as me and if you don't like it, you can go to hell."

Paula was an older woman, probably the oldest woman I ever dated. But because she had been through so much in life I felt like out of all my women, she and I best related. I think because she was eight years my elder she got over a lot on me. But I ain't mad at her. She had game too, so between us there was no animosity.

Paula was off the hook. She was real people. I guess that's why I hung around. She was one of them pretty girls with that down low ghetto style. She was fun. It was nothing serious. I still call her every now and then. But I only call her after a payday when I have money to spend.

After Paula, or maybe it was before, I dated this one chick who had just broken up with her boyfriend of six years. He had hurt her so bad that when she'd talk about him her eyes filled with tears. It's unfortunate when a female has been through a sour relationship because the new fella who's trying to get with her gets the short end of the stick. Not only that, but he gets knocked over the head with it too. I'm referring to Gwen, this girl I once knew.

My buddies called Gwen "The Librarian" which was their slang for the sweet, quiet type. Little did they know that she was one who loved to pick a fight. That's all Gwen had been used to, fighting with her ex-boyfriend. My mother told me if I ever hit a woman, she'd cut off both my hands. So when Gwen would get in my face fussing I would just walk away. Or else I'd be the man and agree with everything she'd say. She wouldn't settle for that. My *nonchalantness* seemed to upset her even more. I didn't need that kind of aggravation in my life. That was for sure.

She used to call me out of name. I'm talking every black bastard in the book. That girl would actually put her hands on me and not to slap the shit out of her, you don't know how much self-control it took. I honestly believe that's exactly what Gwen was trying to push me to. It was like she was deliberately pushing all of my buttons and I didn't find that cool.

I tried to hang in there with Gwen because I understood what she was going through. She had told me things her ex-boyfriend had done to her that no one else knew. For Gwen, being fussed at and hit on was the only attention in a relationship she had received. That is what she expected and therefore tried to precipitate out of me. That just wasn't my steelo, so of course Gwen and I didn't last. There's no way she'll have a future with any man until she can overcome her past.

The past ain't no joke either. That's why I'm afraid to even consider getting married. Just thinking about all the skeletons that might pop out of my closet is scary. Some people say be honest about sexual partners so nothing comes back to haunt. But when a woman says she doesn't care about how many women a man's been with it's a front. That's one of the worse mistakes a man can make, telling a female how many women he's had. And men always fall for the woman's line "Just tell me. I promise I won't get mad."

At first telling her is beneficial because now, out of all the females, she wants to be the best. Sexually, she does things she ain't ever done before in order to pass the test. But all good things come to an end, and when it does look out. A man knows the tornado is on its way when all the woman starts to do is pout.

She'll walk around sighing in anticipation of the man asking her what's wrong. At first she'll say "oh nothing," but the truth will come out before long. Tears will start tripling one by one then she'll start to cry like it's the end of the world. It's an entire three months later but still she says, "I can't believe you've slept with that many girls."

The man will try endlessly to explain to the woman that the other girls didn't mean a thing. That he wasn't really serious about any of them, that most of them were just flings. "That's even worse," is the next thing to come out of the woman's mouth. Then the man just stands there dumb founded realizing that there's no easy way out. After that, the relationship goes down hill, which is really kind of sad. But make note that not once will the woman volunteer the information of how many men she's had.

That's why I love women. They are smart and the most intriguing, appealing and esoteric creatures in the world. I don't know if it comes natural, or if it's instilled in them as girls. Santa's helpers did not create women, so what I'm saying is that they are not toys. They are delicate, and quite untouchable, therefore they shouldn't be put into the hands of little boys.

When it comes to females, there are more flavors than ice cream. Each one has her own taste, no matter how alike some may seem. It's up to the man to educate himself on how different women should be treated. The marathon of running after a woman's heart can be bitter if defeated.

So playas, play your games but make sure you're playing at your best. Beware of the games you play though, because what goes around.....well, you know the rest.

Joylynn M. Jossel

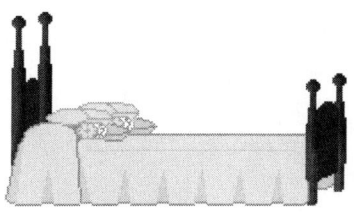

Nothin' Worse Than An Unmade Bed

Joylynn M. Jossel

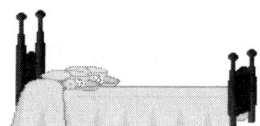

  I'm so tired that I could throw myself onto the bed and fall right to sleep. But hopefully Mel will be home soon and he likes the bed to be nice and neat. "There ain't nothin' worse than an unmade bed," I can hear him saying it now, "I always make the bed, but when I go to get in it, it's messed up some how."

  Mel complains about everything, even the way I squeeze toothpaste out of the tube. Another one of his pet peeves is the way I prepare his food. His meats have to be cooked perfect, right down to the bone. He's so persnickety that when I make tea, he complains if the water boils too long.

  I should have just ignored his complaints but I have a tendency to get so frustrated that I scream and shout. I guess these are just some of the things that being in love's about. And I don't think I could ever stop loving Mel. I've never encountered a kinder man yet. I remember bragging about him to all my friends the very first day we met:

"Today I met a man who will change my life completely. A man who is not afraid to express himself and does nothing secretly. His heart is as warm as marshmallows settling over a hot cup of chocolate. He's so head strong that if his mind sets to do something, nothing can stop it. This man I met has an immeasurable IQ for he speaks with such knowledge. He gained his wisdom from experience and sacrifice, not from some fancy college. He has the personality of a garden of flowers. He has vanquished all the weeds. He is going to be the man to do without to satisfy my needs. This man I met, I will tell you, attracts people from miles around. It's quite impossible for anyone not to hear the calling of his smile. I don't know if he knows it yet, but someday I'm going to be his wife. I'm going to carry on his essence by bearing an identical life. This man I met will identify, correct, and forgive me for my mistakes. I'll never use his love for me against him. I'd never cause him heartbreak. I will do what ever it takes to keep him happy and honest. I will never forge my love, delude him, tell him lies, or break a promise. I feel like a changed person and for him I'll do all that I absolutely can, to become a true and natural woman, because today I met a man."

As a little girl, I had prayed for God to send me someone like Mel. I swore to God that I would love this man dearly and always treat him well. But I wondered how I would know that the man lying next to me would be there when I'd wake, to praise me in times of goodness and to forgive me for my mistakes. Would it be something in his eyes or would it be buried in his heart? Would it feel like something was missing from my life when the two of us were apart? Would our squabbles bring us closer together or would they separate our minds? If I searched high and low, a better love could I find? How do you know that the person lying next to you holds love for you that's true? There are no signs and there are no clues. For some reason you just do.

When a person does find their soul mate, something happens that never again makes life the same. No longer are circumstances taken for granted and every destined affair is conditioned to change. Something happens that makes the soul weep and the spirit chuckle without end. Something happens that when each day concludes it is anticipated zealously for the next to begin. And every breath is much easier to take in and every heart beat sends chills throughout. And something happens that makes the blood rush through the body like water through a spout. Then sometimes there will be intervals when there is nothing to feel, hear, say, or see. But if nothing ever happened again in my life, I'm just glad that Mel happened to me.

Along with my word to God, I vowed to myself to be loving, sweet, and tender. My mother had taught me that these things were characteristics of my gender. She said that a man's pride is worth more to him than a block of solid gold. She said to pretend the man is always right, then it's clemency rather than an appeal when he proves to be wrong. My father had always said that it is the woman's duty to keep peace in the home. My parents have been married for 35 years. They credit their insights for their being together so long.

When I was born my parents named me Promise to remind them of their lifetime commitment. They've had some good times and some bad times, but they have never had any resentment. My parents have presented each other with roles as if they were performing in a stage play. Their acceptance and portrayal of these roles is what has allowed their love to grow more genuine each day.

This was the kind of love I had hoped to share with Mel. There would be those occasions of disagreement but all would end well. Yet, I found myself pushing Mel's love away from me further and further each day. I would snap at him for every little thing he'd do and every little thing he'd say.

Once we were in the mall and we bumped into an old girlfriend of his. Out of politeness he stopped and asked her how she was doing as well as her kids. At the time, of course, I stood their smiling and every so often touching up my hair. On the inside I was steaming mad, but on the outside I looked confident, like I didn't care. After their "good-byes'" and "nice seeing yous'" we headed on down the mall. I was walking like a bull preparing for a brawl.

"Promise, what's wrong?" Mel asked me, "You're acting like you have an attitude."

I stopped dead in my tracks and yelled, "Nothing's wrong with me. What in the hell is wrong with you? How dare you stop and talk to that tramp while I'm standing there looking like a fool. If I bumped into one of my ex-boyfriends in the mall, I wouldn't do that to you!"

That was the first time we had ever had an argument in a public place. I knew he was embarrassed because I could tell by the look on his face. That didn't stop me though. I continued to raise more cane. People walking by were looking at us like we were insane. In a fit of rage I stormed away shouting that I was going home and that I would walk. I figured he'd come after me begging me to calm down so that we could talk.

I headed for the exit door and he caught up with me right before I got there. He handed me a dollar and said, "Just in case your feet get tired here's bus fare." He strolled off and left me standing there and didn't look back once. Even though I thought I was making a fool out of him I ended up being the dunce.

To spite him I began to walk home, but I didn't get very far. He pulled up beside me, gave me a great big smile, and told me to get in the car.

Mel always breaks the ice because he knows that I'm too stubborn to even try. He is opposite of myself, who can hold a grudge until the day I die. Mel believes that people shouldn't hold grudges, that being present is the root of being happy in life. And that being present allows individuals to enjoy the company of their friends, family, children, husband or wife. Mel says that being present is the ability to express ones self on the spot and it is the art of cooling off anxieties before they get too hot. He is an adamant believer that being present alleviates animosity and useless turmoil, and that because issues have been resolved, future encounters are held on fresh soil. And lastly, that being present is healthy to the soul as well as refreshing, and it is a guarantee to ensure tranquillity, peace at mind, and good blessings.

Mel ended up being the one who keeps the peace in our home. I know that is my role, but somewhere down the line I went wrong. I have a short temper and when it flares there's no telling what will come out my mouth. If anything, I'm the one who keeps up the confusion and tension in our house.

It is difficult, still, I try so hard to be careful of the things I say. Sometimes before going to bed at night I even pray:

> *"Now I lay me down to sleep.*
> *I pray to think before I speak.*
> *But if by chance I should forget,*
> *Lord, leave my soul just take my lips."*

Prayer alone though, won't help me. I need to face the facts. Sometimes I can't believe myself, the way I act. One night a few of Mel's friends were over to watch a fight on pay per view. I had made some hors d'oeuvres and bought drinks. Everything seemed cool. The $45 fight ended up lasting only a round or two. The night was still young so the guys wanted to find something to get into. They decided to go to "Eight Ball", which is a spot where people go to shoot pool. Mel planned on going with the guys and leaving me home with nothing to do.

I was angry that Mel wanted to spend time with his friends so without thinking I shouted, "You better not go anywhere." I began to fuss at him right in front of his friends, which is something he didn't think I'd ever dare. I cursed at him. I may have even pushed him. I called him out of his name. His friends eventually left. Mel and I eventually made up, and as always he took the blame.

Later that evening I lay cuddled up under him enjoying the warmth of his breath. Falling asleep without nerve to take the blame, that night like all the rest.

This strait could have only gone on for so long so I can't blame Mel for going away. If only I had not taken his love for granted, I wouldn't be hoping for him to come back to me today. It's been three days since he walked out the door. It's been three days since I've slept. It's been three days since I've last heard his voice. It's been three days that I've wept.

If God brings my man back through that door, this time I am going to love him right. I am going to admire him, respect him, and tell him how much I appreciate him day and night. I am going to bend over backwards to please him only because for me he'd do the same. I'll never humiliate my baby again or call him out of his name.

Who am I kidding? I know I haven't changed overnight. I love Mel with all my heart, but getting back with him wouldn't be right. I can't treat him the way he deserves to be treated so I need to let go and allow him to be with somebody who can. Even though it's going to kill me to know that another woman is pleasing my man.

Mel treated me like gold while I treated him like tarnished bronze. Right now I wish I had a fairy godmother to turn back time with her magic wand.

Black men already receive little respect from people on the streets alone. But it's ridiculous when the black man can't receive respect in his own home.

I want to blame my parents by saying that they raised me in a make believe world. For making me believe that sugar and spice and everything nice was the ingredient of every girl. But they told me love is hard work, still I thought if I really loved someone there'd be nothing to it. I thought I could be a respectful and loving person until it came down to it.

Now I see that maybe it is words that turn a gentle, loving, and sensitive mate into a brute. It is a scurrilous tongue that sucks the sweet juices from a fruit. It is not the black man and woman's culture to be discourteous and ill bred. That is something we bring into being in one another by not being caring, but callous instead. What can one truly accomplish by rendering dialect that is disparaging and discouraging? One should be giving words that are both complimentary and encouraging.

If only I had practiced what I, will now, preach, but I guess I'm learning the hard way. Without the touch, smile, or comfort of Mel, I honestly don't think I can make it a fourth day. This time going out with the girls isn't going to get Mel off of my mind. Something just doesn't feel transitory about his leaving this time. The bad part is, when I was cussing and fussing, I was hurting Mel deliberately and I knew it. All the screaming and shouting was draining his reverence for me, yet I continued to do it.

I can't help but wonder if it is I who has given black women a bad name. Is it me and my scurrilous tongue that are to blame? Is it my actions that put black men into the arms of women who's skin is white? Have I made the black man believe that all black women do is fuss and fight? For the past three days these questions have been constipating my head. So far, I've avoided the obvious answer, by refusing to find myself alone in an unmade bed.

Daddy's Little Girl

Joylynn M. Jossel

    Sometimes, right smack in the middle of the day I can't help but think: "How could my father have done such a horrible thing? What did I do to deserve this besides the fact that I was born? What did I do to make him not love me anymore?" For him to have done such a thing I wonder if he ever loved me from the start. If he did, then how could he have formed the foundation of which aches my heart?

    I wonder if he can stand to look at himself in the mirror each morning he awakes. Before he can consciously proceed with his day I wonder how long it takes. Just how long does it take him to clear his mind of what he did to his little girl? Years later is he at all concerned with how I am now functioning in this crazy world?

    What's so sad is that he hurt me so bad and he probably has no intentions on ever acknowledging it. What he did to me, I may be strong enough now to forgive him for, but it's something I'll never forget.

Sometimes I'm just watching television and out of no where comes the rain. A thundershower of my tears which total three decades of pain. And when they start to fall, there's nothing I can do to keep them from coming. One by one, they drip like drops of water from a faucet left barely running.

I don't know why it has taken so long for me to cry. I guess because before I had nothing but anger inside. But shockingly, all that heated anger has turned into sadness and hurt. I try to hate him all over again but that hasn't seemed to work. Why can't I hate him now when I have hated him for so long? These tears make me feel so weak when I've tried to be nothing but strong.

I feared that shedding a tear would soften the hard thoughts I had worked so hard to create. So to keep out those unwarranted feelings I set up a barrier of hate. I've never wanted to catch myself thinking about him because he didn't deserve to clutter my mind. But now, for some reason, thoughts of him have been lingering on my mind.

It's hard for me to look at myself in the mirror, not because of shame. It's hard because I sometimes think that the person looking back at me is to blame. Maybe I wasn't pretty enough, or better yet, maybe I should have been a boy. Maybe my birth brought him despondency and perplexity versus joy. I don't know what it is that made my father walk out that door. I don't know what I did to make him not want me anymore.

Growing up without him was easy because there's some things a child doesn't understand. In my eyes, his not sticking around didn't make him any less of a man. I was a child and for all I knew he and my mom couldn't get along. I didn't analyze that his leaving her was okay but his leaving me was wrong. Besides, by the time I could walk there was another man in my life. My little sister was his daughter and my mother was his wife.

I was groomed to call him my father by the time I reached the age of two. I didn't know he wasn't my biological father even though everyone else in the family knew. It didn't even dawn on me that everyone else had a caramel complexion. Probably because my dark chocolate skin never brought forth any rejection. And everyone treated me as though my veins pumped the same blood as theirs. But knowing my father, to treat me any different, no one would have dared.

See, the man I grew to know as my father, like any other man, was proud. What he took in as his own he would manage to take care of somehow. He knew it would be difficult getting his family to accept me, but still, he went out on a limb. He made it clear that if anyone mistreated me that they'd have to answer to him. That was my father's way of protecting the situation…he'd have my back if no one else. But no one took into consideration the one day I'd have to fend for myself.

My father's protecting me was a natural gesture, but in reality he wasn't really protecting me at all. Upon learning about my concealed circumstances no one in this world could have broken my fall.

Adults sometimes tend to get into deep conversation when children are around. Because the child is in their own little world they assume the child hasn't heard a sound. In my case some family members were gossiping and my younger cousin over heard. They thought she was too young to understand (maybe she was, but that didn't disable her from repeating every word).

"Did you know you're not really in our family?" I think that's what she said. I was only about nine years old so I can't quite describe what was going through my head. Disbelief, hurt, curiosity, those were just some of my emotions. My cousin's spilling of the beans started causing all kinds of commotion.

I start hearing things like "No matter what, we love you just the same." I was told, "You are part of our family regardless of what anyone might say." No one ever had the guts to just come out and say the truth. So I brushed my cousins comment under the rug throughout the remainder of my early youth.

But as I got older the inevitable came to surface. I had been lied to, mislead, and averted, without malice, but on purpose. My parents sat me down and told me of the choice that they had made. The choice to make me a part of the family simply by branding me with the family name.

I grew distant from everyone. I decided to keep to myself rather than make a fuss. I didn't want anything to do with anybody in the family because in them I couldn't trust. I even questioned whether all along if my sister as well knew. So I separated from the likes of her because I felt she had betrayed me too.

I decided against being nasty or giving everybody a piece of my mind. Instead I kept my feelings to myself in hopes they'd fade away with time. That's when the hate formed for my biological father (the man I never knew). I had put all the blame on my family forgetting that he was a big part of the scandal too.

I imagined him wanting to meet and have lunch with me in some foreign secluded place. Him having the opportunity to beg for forgiveness and me having the opportunity to throw my food in his face. I imagined attending his funeral in all white after receiving notice that he was dead. Not to pay any last respects but to spit on his grave instead. I imagined he had a wife and kids, you know, one big happy family. I got ill at the thought of him caring for them when he never cared for me. I imagined he was probably taking his kids to amusement parks and walking them to school. I imagined him going down in a plane crash so that those children would be without a dad too.

Nothing but hate I had for him. Nothing but hate and anger. Now I find it incongruous that I put that much energy into despising a stranger. So for a few years I totally blocked out the fact that he ever existed. And each time a little part of me wondered of him the bigger part resisted.

I would watch TV talk shows of bastards trying to locate their biological fathers. They'd be crying and snorting and I'd ask myself why anyone in their right mind would even bother. Not once did these shows remind me of my own. Like I said, I hadn't even thought about him in so long.

But here recently I've thought of him more often than ever before. And when I think of him I don't feel that hate and anger anymore. Unlike before, as where I wouldn't allow my feelings to budge, as an adult I've realized that it's time to relinquish the grudge.

I think it's my curiosity that has over ridden the hate. The concern of if it is he of whom I've inherited some of my traits. And there's the void that goes beyond just being mad. It's the not knowing of the brothers and sisters I might have.

I feel similar to that of a person who suspects that their lover is cheating. On the outside I pretend everything is okay while on the inside I'm fatally bleeding. Not knowing, I think, is the most difficult wound to heal. It's halting me from being able to express how I truly feel.

Maybe I'm suppose to be feeling love for other siblings I might have. Maybe he's never told anyone about me, so perhaps I should be feeling sad. Maybe he never even knew I was his so maybe I should be feeling relieved. My mother may not have told him I was even born, so maybe I should feel even more deceived.

Didn't anyone think about me before all these decisions were put into place? I'd rather never been born at all if that's the case. Didn't anyone see the burden they bestowed upon me each time they looked into my eyes? Didn't they know that my body would break down due to the heavy weight of their lies? Did anyone know that I would be the one who'd suffer for his or her mistakes? When they used their hearts to justify my place, did anyone know it was my heart that would break?

I try so many times to put myself in my parent's place back in the day. Abortion wasn't legal here yet, so I guess they felt there was no other way. I would have much rather been a fetus sucked to death through a tube. That way I wouldn't have to deal with some of the things that I now have too.

It hurts. It hurts so badly. It's like a virus without a cure. Not knowing is the worse pain anyone can endure.

How can so many men do this? How can they abandon their child? They don't even have the decency of an animal in the wild. I've watched those series on wildlife and witnessed the look in the lion's eye. The lion will throw himself for kill before he'll let his baby die. The lion is the King he claims to be when it comes to his descendent. He puts the burden of his young before the glory of his own independence. The lion can conceitedly credit himself for the future survival of his offspring. It saddens me that in our human society we lack the presence of far too many Kings.

I am very sad. I am crying. I am hurting deep inside. And every now and then I can't stand to be alive. But I'm here and there's nothing I can do about it now. I am just going to have to keep growing and coping with this some how.

I'm a woman now. I can't dwell on the past so I have to move on with my life. I'm married with three children of my own so I need to focus on being a good mother and a good wife. I can't let negative emotions surface within my home. I am just as adamant about that as I am about keeping headstrong.

Just to make something very clear, the man I know as my dad is someone that others weren't even fortunate enough to have. I wouldn't trade anything to not have him in my life. My heart knows he never set out to hurt me but that he was only trying to do right. The thought of replacing him is something that I could never conceive. The love my father has given me, by any other, couldn't be retrieved.

And as far as hating my biological father, well, I guess that's just not in me anymore. This time the vanishing of my anger is a permanent act for sure. But don't think for a minute I wouldn't give anything in this world...to be able to turn back the hands of time and know what it feels like to be daddy's little girl.

Joylynn M. Jossel

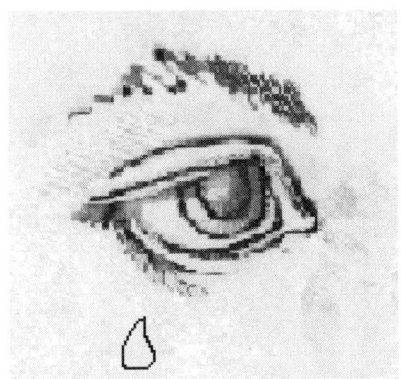

You Ever Seen A Grown Man Cry

Joylynn M. Jossel

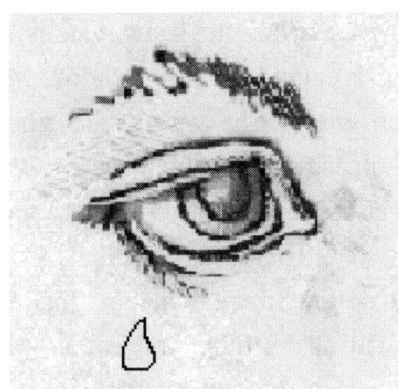

*E*ven though I wake every day to the shine of the sun and the tunes birds sing, I can't seem to get excited about a day that I know ain't got nothin' in store for me. Today someone is going to hit the lottery and someone else is going to fall in love. Anything good happening to me on any day is unheard of.

I hate living. I wish I was dead. I ought to lodge a bullet right through my head. A rope would do, I could kick, twitch, and twist. Even better, I could take a razor blade and watch the blood pour from my wrist. I could crank up the car engine and slowly inhale death, or put the car in full gear and plunge over a cliff. I could take an overdose of pills or put a radio in my bath. I could turn on the stove and blow out the fire leaving only fumes of gas. I've thought of doing such, but each time I've reneged. I figure if I have the courage to self inflict death, then I have the courage to live.

But what in the hell do I have to live for? I have a son that the bitch won't let me see. She's got some man living up in her house and James Jr., my son, is calling that nigga daddy. My boy is five years old and I haven't seen him since he was two. That bitch told me I wasn't no real man when I turned down good jobs to go to school.

The university was going to provide me an education in exchange for me swinging a bat. There was hope that I would become a baseball star and I wanted nothing more than that. That way I would be able to provide my boy with all the things I never had. There would be genuine proudness in his tone when he'd say to his friends, "That's my Dad."

I had my life all mapped out until a drunk driver entered the scene. Some woman, after downing six drinks, totaled my car and totaled my dreams.

Her car hit mine head on when she drove into my lane. The doctors did all they could but said my batting arm would never be the same. I still tried exercising my arm but I only ended up making it worse. In a moments time I had been raped of the quench to my dream's thirst.

Have you ever had a dream, a dream that makes everything be as it should, a dream that makes all that is bad turn good? Have you ever wanted to take this rugged dream into your hand and make it appear as smooth as you possibly can? Did you want to mold it, shape it, and provide it with an intricate base so that the final product of your architecture is present by the expression on your face? Have you ever came close to this dream, a dream that is always present on your mind? Finally, once you approached this dream you realized that it had long died. You ponder over whether this dream could have been saved, if you could have dived into the pool of dreams and conquered the vicious waves. If only this dream had known how hard you tried, to shield it and nurture it, but most importantly, to keep it alive.

I'll never get my hopes up about anything else in life. I know first hand how one can be slapped down when trying to come up right. Everything happens for a reason (I've been told), but what reason could there be? Something better awaits (I hear). It's been three years and ain't shit better happened to me.

I'm still living at home under Mom and Dad's roof while working for minimum wage. I work for a local theater company. I help set and clear the stage. It ain't much, but I get by from paycheck to paycheck. I give my parents money for bills and I mail James, Jr. what ever is left.

My parents are in the process of getting visitation rights to see my son. That way, I'll be able to see him too when all is said and done. I guess my failure hurt his mamma more than she led me to believe. I got so caught up into myself that I forgot about her dreams. She wanted the *American Dream*, and being a man, I was to be the provider. When my dreams failed, I failed with them, leaving no strength to stand strong beside her.

I wish my son's mamma could have just hung in there with me and offered some genuine support. Baseball was to be my life, my bread and butter, and not just some sport. But after the car accident, when it was final that I would never play ball again, she began ridiculing and complaining about "have-nots", which insulted me as a man. She fussed that I was sorry and lazy, that those were the real reasons I had turned down good jobs. She protested that she wouldn't allow her son to grow up to be like me, a good for nothing slob. She said that the whole baseball dream was a scam, a disguise, and a fantasy I tried to make true. I started retaliating with my physical strength, which is something I never thought I'd do. Man, I don't blame her for wanting me out of her life. But keeping me from my son, Man that shit ain't right.

Not being able to see my son kills me softly day by day. Not being able to tell him I love him hurts in the worst of ways. The saying that every boy needs a man in his life is not true. Every boy needs a daddy in his life. Not just any man will do. Sometimes I think I could kill that bitch for depriving me of my son. Even more so, for depriving him of all his daddy's love.

I don't understand it. James, Jr. is my boy. As much as he is hers, he's mine. I deserve to hear him when he's laughing and comfort him when he's crying.

How come when a child is taken from its birth mother everyone knows how she feels? When a man is forbidden to have contact with his child his emotions are just as real. Men tend not to show their emotions because we are suppose to be made of steal. I'm not one to cry and whine. I hold my shit inside because I've learned how to deal. I ain't never seen no grown man cry and I ain't gonna be the first. Before I let anything bring me to tears, I'll die first.

Women think that shit is cute, keeping a father from his child. If the father is such a no good nigga, then why did the ho lay down? He's still the same no good nigga she was fucking every night. Women put themselves in that "single mother" category instead of the category of a wife. But society wants to blame the male by labeling him a "dead beat dad". Meanwhile the baby is in the middle of this bullshit, damn it's so sad. Bitches talkin' bout they can survive without the aid of any man. Yet they are readily collecting at the first of each and every month from Uncle Sam.

I don't mean to sound so negative towards the female species because some of them are straight. I might have a more positive outlook if I had only had the patience to wait. You see, when old girl and me (my son's mother) hooked up we were freshmen in high school. She had given birth to James, Jr. by the time our sophomore year was through.

At first she ganked money from me for a termination procedure and premeditated changing her mind. Then I found out she had slept with my best friend of 12 years, which planted doubts of whether James Jr. was really mine. I thought I was in love though, come to find that the shit was only part-time bliss. She was my world, my first love, my first sexual experience, and she was even my very first kiss. My feelings were beyond infatuation, I was taking my place up to bat as a man. I had created a beautiful being with a beautiful woman of whom I much adored back then.

We both completed high school, but old girl is the only one who's attending college. At this stage in my life, fuck a professor and a book. For my survival I feed off street knowledge. Don't go stereotyping. I ain't into no illegal things. I'm talkin' 'bout the kind of knowledge that kickin' it with the old playas bring.

So many young folks don't want to hear the elders, they want to experience everything first hand. If I had only been listening a little earlier in life, I probably wouldn't be in the predicament I'm in.

I was told to take my time, not to grow up so fast, but to enjoy the offerings of life. I was told to worry about making love and making babies after making a home for me and my wife. I didn't hear anybody though. My life had been all planned out by me. But when confronted by the realist of reality, I was left standing dumbfounded and ignorant of a plan "B".

No matter how many failures I was destined, because of my son, I would always have a reason to live. And to have my boy back in my life there is nothing I wouldn't give. I would tell James Jr. each day how much love I have for him inside. If I had my boy in my life I would have such infinite pride.

But what if the courts say that my parents can't have him around me? What if they say I have no rights? What if they say I'm a no good loser? I can't risk losing this fight. I wish his mamma would just die. I know that's a horrible thing to say. But if she were dead I'd have my boy for good that way. I could wake him each morning and get him ready for school. I could take him to ball games, you know, do the things daddies do.

If I ever see my son again the sad part is that he won't even know I'm his father. She's probably poisoned his mind with foul thoughts against me, so I probably shouldn't bother. She's probably filled him with lies telling him I ain't shit; that I didn't want him from the start. She's going to make it as hard as possible for me to win his heart. But what if her tactics work and James, Jr. won't even want to see my face? What if she has already programmed him to feel nothing for me but disgrace? When his mamma took him out my life, she took the biggest part of me. It's been three long years, I can't continue to just let this craziness be.

All this shit is constipating my mind...I'm going fucking crazy. The world is spinning like mad and reality is becoming fatally hazy. That's it! What do I have to lose? My descendant, against me, has already be tainted. These four walls of insanity inside my head, for my arrival, have been freshly painted. It's time for me to do what I have to do, like a warrior I resort to my gun. Beads of sweat dance wildly upon my forehead as I prepare to orchestrate *just cause* to inherit my son.

As I look into the barrel of this automatic, I, for a half split second, think: "What will become of my son's life if to this massacre I am linked?" That half split second is the last time I will ever be James Senior again. After that I will have become a stranger to myself...an unknown mad man.

Though my no-name brand tennis shoes are made with the softness of rubber. I can hear each step as, from my own body, I depart further and further. Are you with me? Yeah, you. I want you to feel exactly how I'm feeling this very moment. I want you to sympathize not empathize if you had a lifetime dream, but then circumstances stole it.

Look down at your heart. See it beating right out of your chest? In goes a hand to rip it right out leaving a vulgar mess. Now your brain hurts. The sledgehammer in it is impossible to remove. The stitches holding your spine in place have just burst, so there goes your backbone too. Still with me? Good, because I need you with me the rest of the way now. Me and you, us, we are going to pull this slaying off somehow. Please don't you abandon me. Stay with me until the end. I'm no longer fiction. I'm inside of you. I'm that clandestine nature within.

It's five o'clock in the morning so the sun has yet shown up for its shift. I'm so confounded that my legs barely work so I need you to give me a lift. Her house is not that far, as a matter of fact, a couple more blocks and we're there. I'm blank. I'm emotionless. So to answer your question, hell no I ain't scared.

I can only think about my son, my child, my baby, the one that bitch stripped me of. This slaying is not out of hate or anger. This shit is out of love.

Enough of that. Now that we're here should we knock on the door or forcefully intrude? I've got it, let's go to her bedroom window and immediately let shots ring through.

I'm glad that you are still here for me. I thought that I would have to go through this alone. Your lack of restraint confirms that at this particular moment in time you don't see this act as wrong.

POP, POP, POP, POP, POP!

There's no rap song or movie about the ghetto to blame. It's the insanity of trying to fit this world's definition of sane.

Let's go! Let's go! We did it! Run! Run as fast as a human can. With each step the gun becomes the weight of a cannon, trying to slip through the sweat of the hand. Don't look back! Keep running!

We're almost home where we'll be safe. Don't worry, no one will have a clue as to the assailant, we didn't leave a trace.

Do you hear that? What is that thump? It's heartbeats. Damn it's loud. Out of breath, but just keep running. Home is not much further now.

True reality hits as I lay in the middle of the floor gasping for one last breath. I'm wondering if the shit that's playing in my head is real or if it's Memorex. The volume on the television is tuned higher than the devil's calls. No sooner than I drift into a shallow sleep I'm enclosed permanently by the previously mentioned four walls.

> "Good Morning. I'm Kayla Williams here at WTVG News. And our top story of the day may be quite disturbing to you. At about 5 a.m. shots rang out at 1372 Grodgen Place. Five shots were fired into the bedroom window and the assailant fled without a trace. The names of the victims have not been released. We are waiting for the families to be notified by the Columbus police. We don't have much detail to give you, but the word is that two are dead. A 21 year-old woman and her five year-old boy laid cuddled in her bed."

As I wake, I wonder why I had this nightmare, if an underlying message accompanied the fear. I wonder if nightmares are warnings that eternal destruction is soon near. I had often thought that nightmares were the foundation for the caged personality. Nightmares, I suppose, allow during sleep what is banned from reality. I don't know, but this nightmare seemed uncannily real. I was hearing things I could hear and I was feeling things I could feel. I was doing shit I could do and I was saying shit I could say. Maybe that nightmare was my cue, my foretoken that today is to be the day.

No longer a nightmare, I'm looking into the barrel of this black, cannon like, automatic. My fucked up life keeps spiraling through my head...I can't take this shit anymore. I've had it!

Above all the shit though, is a vision of my boy's face. That's just one last thing I'll crave and never be able to taste. My veins are popping and it feels as if my mind is about to explode. My head is tired of all the tears, for over the years, it's had to hold.

You ever seen a grown man cry? You ever seen that look in his eye? Than to let that first tear drop he'd rather die. He can't keep the others from flowing no matter how hard he tries. Following these drops are arrays of "whys". His weep lasts forever as time goes by. Your witnessing shrinks him to the size of a fly. I don't mean to get personal and I don't mean to pry. Just wondering if you ever seen a grown man cry.

POP!

"How long will we continue to wait at the end of the rainbow before realizing that we, in fact, are the pot of gold?"

Joylynn M. Jossel

It's All About Joy!!!

The newest author to hit the literary scene is Joylynn Meleke Jossel, born August 12, 1971 and a native of Columbus, Ohio. She is the virginity of writing. Her style is untouchable. Joy's ("All of my friends call me Joy," she states. "After reading my works, my readers will know me in as much depth as my friends do. It only seems right to be on a first name basis with *them…my readers…my friends.*") first published title, Please Tell Me If The Grass Is Greener, is absolutely peerless of its kind. Her style of writing is being referred to as "Poefiction". It takes you beyond poetry, prose and the standard short story.

"Poefiction" is sweeping the nation. It tells a story in such a flow that it prohibits the reader from finding a stopping point. So when informed that you won't be able to put Joy's book down once you begin reading it, take heed. It is undisputedly catchy.

A month before the official April 30th 2001 release of her paperback title, Joy was featured in the Third Annual Spirited Sisters Expo Author's Corner in Columbus, Ohio. She then went on to autograph copies of her book at the 2001 Annual Spring Kappa Wine Sip and performed a reading/signing at the African American Heritage Festival, Media Play North and Ujamaa Bookstore in Columbus, Ohio. Joy sold out of copies at her book signings in New Orleans during the Essence Music Festival and represented Columbus, Ohio at the 2001 Harlem Book Fair and Black Book Expo 2001 in Brooklyn, NY. Joy was proud to be the producer and host of the Procter & Gamble River Front Classic and Jamboree Poetry Jam 2001 in Cincinnati, Ohio. In addition, Joy performed poetry and signed copies of her book at the 2001 Black Writers Reunion and Conference in Dallas, Texas. When her title debuted she received a wonderful write up in the Columbus Post, the Monday Morning Word Magazine and was interviewed live on WCLL TV 19. Joy's book was the first to be featured in the www.defpoetryjam.com online store.

Joy grew up in the North Linden area of Columbus, Ohio so she definitely reaches out to readers in that area. "I want to first share my gift of writing with the community wherein I based my writing experiences," says Joy. She hopes to do so by holding readings/signings at the Columbus Metropolitan public library branches and college campus bookstores and libraries in her community. Joy began reaching her goal when she was invited to address the adult reader's book club at the Martin Luther King Jr. library branch in Columbus, Ohio. As a graduate of Columbus State Community College, where she received her Associates of Arts, and Capital University, where she received her Bachelor of General Studies, those two colleges are sure to be on her agenda.

In addition to her reading/signing at the African American Heritage Festival in Columbus, Ohio, Joy volunteered to do crafts with the children during the event. "Children are always drawn to my reading/signing set up because of the colors of the rainbow and the pot filled with Anthony Thomas chocolate gold foiled coins," states Joy. "I've made it a point to have something available to show the children I appreciate and desire to maintain their interest." Joy assisted the children in designing bookmarks with their names on it followed by the words "I AM THE GOLD". I want to start instilling this in the young minds now, says Joy, "and I can't think of a better way to do so."

Joy is always trying to find a way to instill the importance of literacy in the youth. "As an alumni and 12 year volunteer of I KNOW I CAN (a college access program assisting and preparing Columbus Public school students for college), I am obligated to remain a member of *the village*," she says.

Joy also shows her dedication to literacy and education through MYRA (Minority Youth Recognition Awards). She has volunteered and shown support for this program that takes one night out of each year (for the last 12 years) to recognize and celebrate the achievements of the minority youths in her community. "The MYRA ceremony is a birth celebration of the mind," says Joy. "If we can celebrate birthdays and holidays, then we can celebrate the mind."

About ten years ago is when Joy first realized her gift of writing. She began digging up and compiling all of her writings, which included everything from elementary journal entries to rainy day writings. She eventually pieced together a children's story of which she convinced her employer, Century Surety Company, to allow her to produce copies using company equipment and supplies. Without hesitation her company abided and several copies of the children's story, <u>Annabella and the Castle Belonging to the Troll</u>, was distributed to all fifth graders at Linden Elementary School (Joy's former elementary school). She did not stop there. Within her treasure she found a poem she had written to help her son learn the months of the year. Again, her employer allowed her to produce hundreds of copies of the poem. This poem was distributed to every CMACAO Head Start student in her community and used in each classroom as well.

"From countless episodes of the Oprah Winfrey show I learned that one's passion is something they would do 24/7 for free. The code to affording to live out one's passion is finding a way to earn money for doing something you would, otherwise, do for free," says Joy. "I knew I couldn't rely upon my employer forever to allow me to utilize office equipment and supplies to get my work to my people."

That is when Joy formed END OF THE RAINBOW projects, Inc. END OF THE RAINBOW is a company founded by Joy. Although the company was given its name in 1998 and not incorporated with the Ohio Secretary of State until 2000, it had been ten years in the making.

Joy's sole purpose with END OF THE RAINBOW was to introduce in all those she encountered the quality of sharing her grandmother instilled in her. "But first," Joy states, "we must all ask ourselves how long will we continue to wait at the end of the rainbow before realizing that we, in fact, are the pot of gold?" This query, now the aphorism for END OF

THE RAINBOW, incites those with a passion in life to envision and manifest it, and for those unaware of their passion to unearth it.

END OF THE RAINBOW has rights to <u>Please Tell Me If The Grass Is Greener</u>. The success of her work is the foundation of the empire that will eventually be reigned by the passions of many others.

As Founder and President of END OF THE RAINBOW, Joy has committed to taking her own passion of writing and making it the exemplar of the company's mission.

> *MISSION STATEMENT: To take the gifted passion assigned to us by God, recognize it, accept it, and act on the fact that the finished package is not ours to keep.*

END OF THE RAINBOW has been blessed in attracting individuals (who Joy refers to as her gold coins) whose hearts were already conversant with the quality of sharing. Each arrived at the tent with the identical mentality and excitement of fostering, utilizing, and advantaging from what one another had to offer. The eventual goal is to be made up of a rainbow of individual projects ultimately forming one big pot of gold.

Joy has so much to share with her readers. In the future she plans to focus on her children's stories. Joy has several completed children's stories in her pot already that are waiting to be put in book format (<u>Anabella and the Castle Belonging to the Troll</u>, <u>The Secret Olivia Told Me</u>, <u>When the Clock Strikes Eight</u>, <u>Oh Brother-Little Brother</u> and <u>What Isaiah pretends to be</u>. Her 13-year-old son is most excited about her children's pieces, as he will be the illustrator for the books and promotions. For now, reading the stories to his little sister, Joy's toddler daughter, will have to suffice.

Joy also has a large compilation of poems highlighting the past decade of her life, which she refers to as <u>World On My Shoulders.</u> Joy will break down the pile into individual books of poetry (Volume I: <u>World On My Shoulders</u>, Volume II: <u>Fallen Bird</u> and Volume III: <u>Flower In My Hair</u>). Joy is also collaborating on an erotica piece of which her contribution will be titled <u>Daydreaming</u>. She has been gifted and blessed, indeed, to be able to touch upon so many genres of writing.

Joy has quite a bit of fruit to savor and wishes she could have one huge feast. But as a self published author, the time and money it takes Joy to get her work out there takes even that much more time and money. "I don't have a problem waiting," Joy says. "The Creator has this all mapped out for me. I'm just following the yellow brick road and meeting so many insightful characters along the way."

Joy is a member of the Black Writers Alliance (BWA), the preeminent organization for Black writers online and offline. "Da family (members of the writing group) have guided me to becoming a successful self published author," states Joy. "I would not have been able to manifest my own vision if it weren't for the vision of Tia Shabazz (BWA's founder)."

But back in 1998, long before Joy stumbled upon BWA and her book distributor, Baker & Taylor, she was distributing her title in report format (8 ½" x 11" pages bound between two paper protectors and a plastic comb) from her brief case. "All I knew is that I had something. I had *it*," Joy proclaims. "I had finally discovered GOLD. God had chosen me to take credit for some powerful pieces of work. It was up to me to polish it up and make it shine."

"There was absolutely no shame in my game," Joy states in regards to selling her book in report format. Nick (Bang), Angie, Steph, Ayanna, Jawan, Dad, Uncle Rudy, Ga-Ga, Kevin, Rinard, Tonya, Cheryl and other family members and friends of Joy had no shame either. They each acted as Joy's book distributor by putting the word out and hustling the books as well. "I could not have been blessed with a greater group of supporters," Joy adds. "Even my hairdresser of 14 years, Terri Deal, put the word out about my book in the beauty shops (and everybody knows word of mouth in the beauty shop is PRICELESS!)."

Joy was more than proud to finally see her book in paperback format. She soon learned, though, that books are, indeed, judged by their cover. Although her book displayed wonderful photographs taken by her personal photographer, Darett Barber, it just didn't seem to jump out at book seekers. In working with a next to nothing budget, Joy couldn't afford to get her book printed in color. She couldn't afford repackaging her product so her book would therefore have to stand on its contents alone, which is quite risky.

"God sent her my way," Joy says about Nancy Flowers Wilson, author of the best selling novel, A Fool's Paradise, and founder of the successful Flowers in Bloom Publishing Company. Joy met the Flower Goddess herself during a book signing that had been arranged by a mutual friend and fellow author, Marlon Green (Making Love in the Rain), who is also owner of Peek-A-Boo Books in Laurel, MD. After watching Joy's intense encounters in persuading perspective readers to buy this generic looking, but powerful piece of work, Nancy knew she had to step in.

"In the middle of the signing," Joy states, "Nancy pulled me to the side and told me that I was a phenomenal woman and that my book was phenomenal and she was not going to allow me to push that generic looking package of which my written words were enclosed. She asked me how I expected anyone to contemplate my book title if I didn't even show some green grass to think about in the first place. I was neither offended nor were my feelings hurt in the least bit because, for one; I was thinking her words but was in denial refusing to verbalize or even ask others what they thought about my bland packaging, for two; I knew I had met a genuine person who would tell me the truth yesterday, today and tomorrow, and three; hell, she reigns from Brooklyn, NY....I mean she could have used the "F" word and really let me have it."

Nancy took on the repackaging of <u>Please Tell Me If The Grass Is Greener</u> as her own personal project. This profound repackaging, of which the result is in your hands, put the book on shelves of bookstores who had originally declined to carry copies of the first printing. Nancy's expertise on *The Power of Packing* successfully both complimented Darett's captivating and lively photography and aided Joy's written words in making this book a BEST SELLER!

ORDER YOUR AUTOGRAPHED COPY OF
PLEASE TELL ME IF THE GRASS IS GREENER
At the low cost of $10 each

This best selling title makes a wonderful gift

Your Name: _____

Address: _____

_____

Phone: _____

Desired Quantity: _____

Add $1 Shipping and Handling per book

Total Enclosed $ _____

Make check or money order payable and mail to:
END OF THE RAINBOW projects
P.O. Box 298238
Columbus, OH 43229

ATTENTION: Bookstores, Book Clubs and Libraries
Receive deep discount from publisher for bulk orders of five or more

[ ] autographed   [ ] plain copy

5 copies-$35 includes shipping and handling
10 or more copies at the cost of $6 per book (includes shipping and handling)

Quantity Ordered _____   TOTAL ENCLOSED $ _____

Ship to: _____

_____

_____

Thank you for your order